A BEDTIME STORY

written by Mem Fox
illustrated by Sisca Verwoert

BOOKSHELF

PUBLISHED BY

MULTIMEDIA INTERNATIONAL (U.K.) Ltd

and in Australia and New Zealand by

HORWITZ GRAHAME Pty Ltd

in association with

Ashton Scholastic

EXCLUSIVE DISTRIBUTORS:

U.S.A.
Scholastic Inc.
730 Broadway
New York, N.Y. 10003
U.S.A.

United Kingdom,
Eire, Europe
Stanley Thornes (Publishers) Ltd
Old Station Drive
Leckhampton
Cheltenham GL53 ODN
England

Australia
Ashton Scholastic Pty Ltd
P O Box 579, Gosford, New South Wales 2250
Also in Brisbane, Melbourne, Adelaide Perth

Canada
Scholastic TAB Publications, Ltd
123 Newkirk Road
Richmond Hill L4C 3G5
Ontario, Canada

New Zealand
Ashton Scholastic Ltd
165 Marua Rd.
Panmure Auckland, 6 New Zealand

ISBN 0 7253 0807 9
Series (Stage 2) ISBN 0 7253 0806 0

Copyright © 1986 text: Mem Fox
Copyright © 1986 illustrations: Sisca Verwoert
Consultants: Robert Andersen & Associates and Snowball Educational
Printed and bound in Hong Kong by Dai Nippon (HK) Ltd

1 2 3 4 5 6 7 8 9 10 11 12
89 90 91

Once upon a time there was a little girl called Polly who had a friend called Bed Rabbit.

Polly and Bed Rabbit had books here, books there, books and stories everywhere. Bed Rabbit couldn't read, so one night when Polly wanted to hear a story she called out, "Mum! Dad! Will someone read Bed Rabbit a story please?"

Dad was planning a holiday and Mum was reading a detective story. Mum looked at Dad. Dad looked at Mum.

"It's your turn," said Dad. "I read to her last night."

"Have you brushed your teeth?" Mum
called out. And quietly carried on reading.

"Yes, I've brushed my teeth," replied
Polly, "and so has Bed Rabbit."

"Have you been to the loo?" Mum called
out. And quietly carried on reading.

"Yes, I've been to the loo," replied Polly, "and so has Bed Rabbit."

"Have you got your pyjamas on?" Mum
called out. And quietly carried on reading.

"Yes, I've got my pyjamas on," replied
Polly, "and so has Bed Rabbit."

"Are you all snuggled in and ready?" Mum
called out. And quietly carried on reading.

"Yes, I'm all snuggled in and ready," replied
Polly, "and so is Bed Rabbit."

"All right, I'm coming!" called out Mum,
who had just got to the most exciting part of
her book. "Would you like a hot-water bottle?"
Mum called out, still reading.

"Yes, please," replied Polly, "and so would Bed Rabbit."

Dad put on the kettle for the hot-water bottle while Mum just quietly went on reading. Dad filled the hot-water bottle and put it on top of Mum's book.

"Isn't anyone coming?" Polly called out.

"Yes, I'm coming," said Mum, putting down her book at last. She picked up the hot-water bottle and went into Polly's room. There were books here, books there, books and stories everywhere.

"Here's your hot-water bottle," Mum said,
as she sat down on Polly's bed. "Now which
story would you like?"

"This is the one that Bed Rabbit wants," said Polly, and she handed her mum the story with the scary pictures.

"Once upon a time . . ." began Mum.

GHOST STORIES

GHOST STORIES

And she carried on reading until they all lived happily ever after.

"Please read it again," begged Polly. "It makes Bed Rabbit feel scared inside."

So Mum read it again.

When she closed the book, Polly and Bed Rabbit were fast asleep. Mum kissed them both and left the room on tiptoe.

Mum sat down in her big chair again. Dad made her a cup of coffee. And they both quietly carried on reading.

Titles in Stage 2:

A Bedtime Story   Mem Fox
A Giant's Cake and other poems   Anne Hanzl,
    Yevonne Pollock, Diane Snowball
An Introduction to Australian Spiders   Esther Cullen
And Billy Went Out to Play   Bronwen Scarffe
Everyone Knows about Cars   Yevonne Pollock
Floating and Sinking   Honey Andersen
Hospitals   Robyn Green
How to Cook Scones   Bronwen Scarffe
I Can Do It   Barbara Comber
I Love Cats   Marjorie-Mary Hurst
It Didn't Frighten Me   Janet L Goss & Jerome C Harste
One Hot Summer Night   Greg Mitchell
Silly Willy   Anne Hanzl
The Greedy Goat   Faye Bolton
The Old Man's Mitten   Yevonne Pollock
When the King Rides By   Margaret Mahy
Where Does the Wind Go?   Marcia Vaughan
Whose Toes and Nose Are Those?   Marcia Vaughan

(*The Greedy Goat*, *The Old Man's Mitten* and *When the King Rides By* are available in small and large formats.)

Other resources in Stage 2 include a Teacher's Resource Book and Audio Bookshelf.

about the author:

Mem Fox is a writer, a teacher, a storyteller, a mother, a wife and a self-confessed bossy-boots who lives in Adelaide. She is the author of the best-selling *Possum Magic*, and of *Zoo-looking* which also is published in Bookshelf.

about the illustrator:

Sisca Verwoert was born in Holland in 1948. She came to Australia as a child and has lived overseas for about ten years of her adult life. She is a painter, an illustrator, a reader and a television watcher, and is currently responsible for three children and a dog.

ISBN 0 7253 0807 9
Series (Stage 2) ISBN 0 7253 0806 0

BOOKSHELF